# FOR TOM SGOUROS

Clarion Books

3 Park Avenue, 19th Floor, New York, New York 10016

Text and illustrations © 1991 by David Wiesner

The illustrations were executed in watercolor on Arches paper.

The text was set in Bulmer.

Book design by Carol Goldenberg.

For information about permission to reproduce selections from this book, write to trade.permissions@hmhco.com or to Permissions, Houghton Mifflin Harcourt Publishing Company, 3 Park Avenue, 19th Floor, New York, New York 10016.

Clarion Books is an imprint of Houghton Mifflin Harcourt Publishing Company.

www.hmhco.com

*Library of Congress Cataloging-in-Publication Data*

Wiesner, David.

Tuesday / written and illustrated by David Wiesner.

p.  cm.

Summary: Frogs rise on their lily pads, float through the air, and explore nearby houses while their inhabitants sleep.

[1. Frogs—Fiction] I. Title.

PZ7.W6367Tu  1991   90-39358

[E]—dc20  CIP  AC

ISBN 978-0-395-55113-4

ISBN 978-0-395-87082-2 (pb)

Manufactured in China

SCP 60  59

4500730841

# TUESDAY

## DAVID WIESNER

### CLARION BOOKS

Houghton Mifflin Harcourt • Boston   New York

TUESDAY EVENING, AROUND EIGHT.

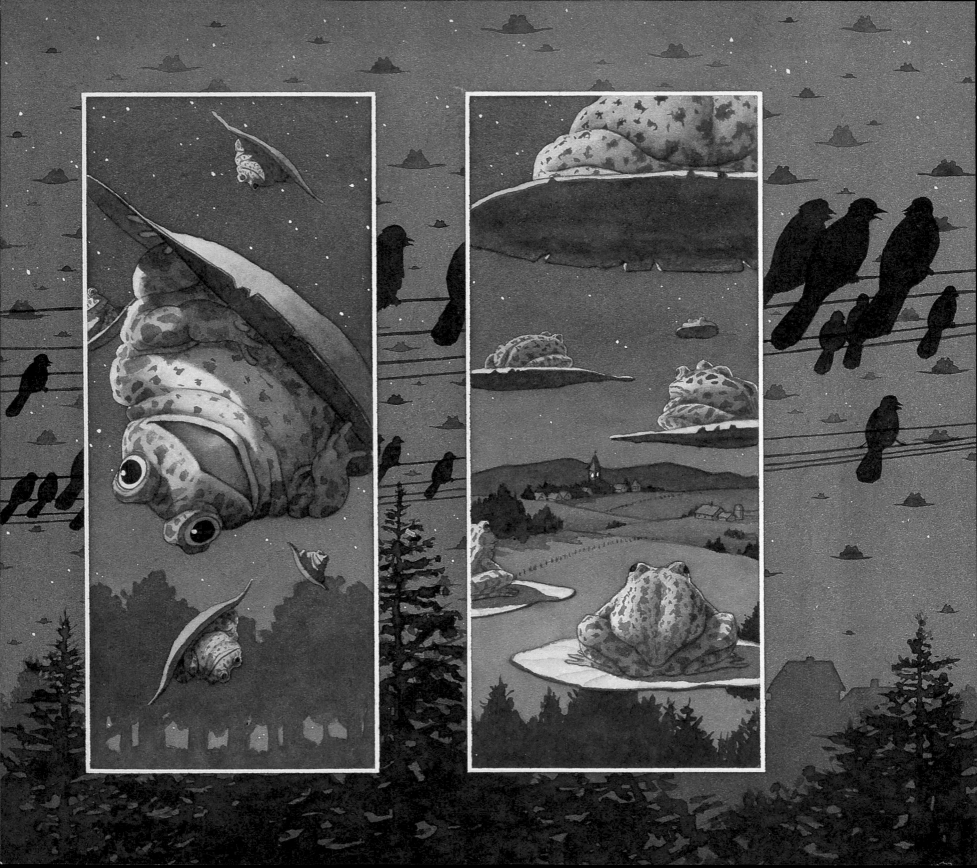

11:21 P.M.

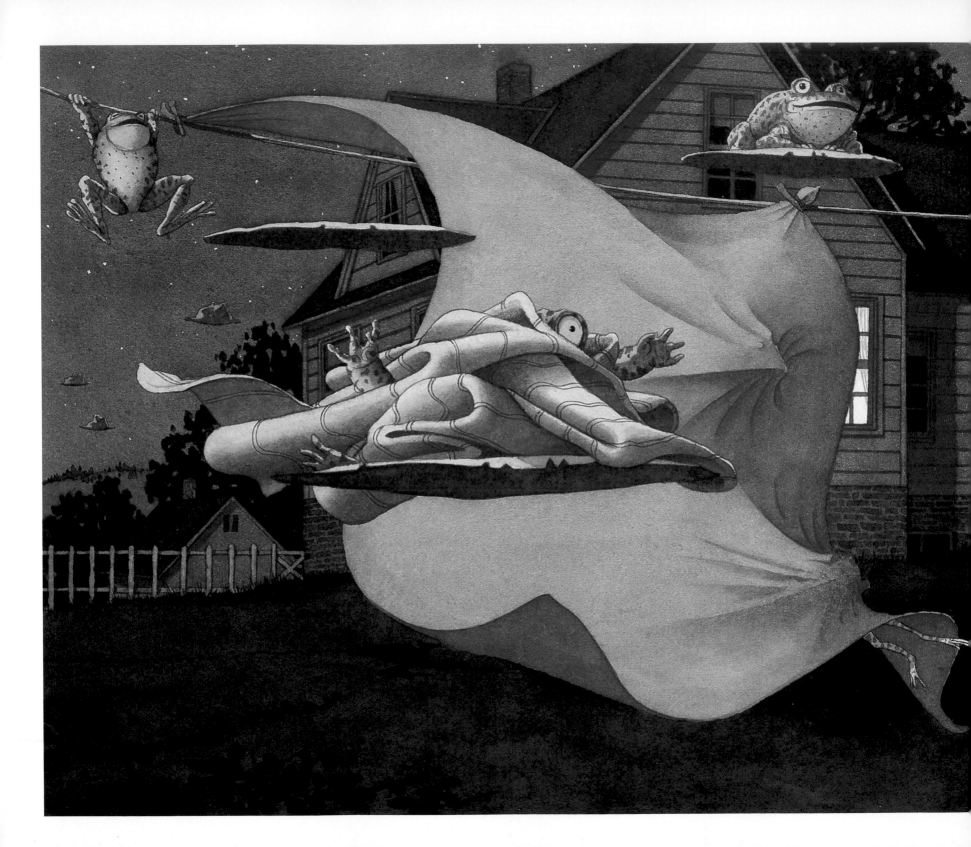

4:38 A.M.

NEXT TUESDAY, 7:58 P.M.